EVER FALLEN IN LOVE

URSULA
RODEL

SCHWEIZERISCHES NATIONALMUSEUM / SWISS NATIONAL MUSEUM
STURM & DRANG PUBLISHERS

URSULA

Mit ihrem Label *Thema Selection* gehört Ursula Rodel (1945 – 2021) zu den Modepionierinnen der Schweiz. Sie entwirft für die emanzipierte, berufstätige Frau – ein Novum in den frühen 70er-Jahren. Ihre Kontakte führen sie von Zürich nach Paris und Rom, wo sie beim Film neue Herausforderungen findet und Freundschaften knüpft. Die Polaroidkamera ist ihr Mittel zur Selbstreflexion und zur Dokumentation ihres Lebens.

ELISABETH

Elisabeth Bossard (1947 – 2008) ist das grosse Verkaufstalent im Laden von *Thema Selection*. Sie hat Stil und Klasse, wie niemand sonst. Gewandt und schön bewegt sich die langjährige Freundin von Filmproduzent This Brunner im Glamour der Filmwelt. Sie ist mit Ursula Rodel auch privat eng befreundet; die beiden gehen auf Reisen und verbringen unbeschwerte, wilde Ferien zusammen.

EDWIGE

Die Französin Edwige Belmore (1957 – 2015) gilt als die Punk-Ikone von New York und Paris der späten 70er- und 80er-Jahre. Sie ist Model, Türsteherin und Sängerin. Ursula Rodel begegnet ihr während ihren Aufenthalten in Paris, als sie für den Film arbeitet. Belmores Androgynität und Unabhängigkeit entsprechen Rodels Lebensstil. Ihre Beziehung ist intensiv und von kurzer Dauer.

DANIEL

Der Schweizer Regisseur Daniel Schmid (1941 – 2006) ist wie Ursula Rodel in einem Hotelbetrieb aufgewachsen. Für seine Ausbildung geht er nach Berlin, wo er erstmals offen seine Homosexualität leben kann. Für das Kostümdesign seines Films *Violanta* 1977, engagiert er Rodel und öffnet ihr die Türen zum internationalen Filmbusiness. Schmid selbst sagt, dass er am Set am liebsten mit Frauen zusammenarbeite.

REGINA

Regina alias Nina Stähli (1950 – 1991) gehört neben Irene Staub zu den bevorzugten Models von *Thema Selection*. In den späten 70er-Jahren lebt die grossgewachsene Schönheit mit der beeindruckenden, dunklen Haarpracht mit Ursula Rodel zusammen. Parallel dazu führt Nina die Beziehung zu Edi Stöckli (1945), Filmproduzent und Vater ihrer gemeinsamen Tochter Zoë (1975), weiter.

IRENE

Irene Staub (1952 – 1989) alias *Lady Shiva*, ist Edelprostituierte, Sängerin, Model und Muse. Sie beeinflusst Ursula Rodel seit ihrem ersten Zusammentreffen in den frühen 70er-Jahren. Irene wird Rodels Freundin und wichtigste Muse. Es ist, als ob Rodel nur für sie entwerfen würde. Ihre erotische Erscheinung öffnet Irene die Türen zu einem flüchtigen, glamourösen Leben, wo sie auf David Bowie, Andy Warhol, Mike Jagger und Federico Fellini trifft.

CATHERINE

Mit der französischen Filmschauspielerin Catherine Deneuve (1943) verbindet Ursula Rodel eine langjährige, innige Freundschaft. Die beiden lernen sich 1978 am Set kennen, wo Rodel Deneuves Garderobe für den Film *Ecoute Voir* entwirft. Weitere Filme folgen. Rodel begleitet ihre Freundin an verschiedene Drehs und in die Ferien. Catherine Deneuve kleidet sich bei *Thema Selection* ein und trifft sich mit Ursula Rodel in Zürich.

URSULA

With her *Thema Selection* label, Ursula Rodel (1945–2021) is one of Switzerland's fashion pioneers. She designs for the emancipated, working woman – a novelty in the early 1970s. Her contacts take her from Zurich to Paris and Rome, where she finds new challenges and makes friends in the film business. The Polaroid camera is a tool for self-reflection and documentation of her life.

ELISABETH

Elisabeth Bossard (1947–2008) is the great sales talent in the *Thema Selection* store. She has style and class like no one else. Elegant and beautiful, the longtime girlfriend of film producer This Brunner moves in the glamor of the film world. She is also close friends with Ursula Rodel in her private life; the two go on trips and spend carefree, wild vacations together.

EDWIGE

French born Edwige Belmore (1957–2015) is considered the punk icon of New York and Paris in the late 70s and 80s. She is a model, bouncer and singer. Ursula Rodel meets her during her stays in Paris when she is working on costumes for film productions. Belmore's androgyny and independence match Rodel's lifestyle. Their relationship is intense and short-lived.

DANIEL

Like Ursula Rodel, Swiss film director Daniel Schmid (1941–2006) grew up in a hotel business. For his education, he goes to Berlin, where he can live his homosexuality openly for the first time. For the costume design of his film *Violanta* (1977), he hires Rodel and opens her the doors to the international film business. Schmid states, that he prefers to work with women on the set.

REGINA

Regina aka Nina Stähli (1950–1991) is one of *Thema Selection's* favorite models, along with Irene Staub. In the late 1970s, the tall beauty with the impressive dark hair lived with Ursula Rodel for a while. At the same time, Nina continues her relationship with Edi Stöckli (1945), film producer and father of their daughter Zoë (1975).

IRENE

Irene Staub (1952–1989) alias *Lady Shiva*, is a high-class prostitute, singer, model and muse. She has influenced Ursula Rodel since their first meeting in the early 1970s. Irene becomes Rodel's friend and most important muse. It's as if Rodel was designing just for her. Her erotic appearance opens the doors to a volatile, glamorous life for Irene, where she meets David Bowie, Andy Warhol, Mike Jagger and Federico Fellini.

CATHERINE

Ursula Rodel and French film actress Catherine Deneuve (1943) have enjoyed a long and close friendship. The two met on a film set in 1978, where Rodel designed Deneuve's wardrobe for the film *Ecoute Voir*. Other films follow. Rodel accompanies her friend on various shoots and vacations. Catherine Deneuve dresses at *Thema Selection* and meets Ursula Rodel in Zurich.

BUZZCOCKS

Ever Fallen In Love (With Someone You Shouldn't 've?)

You spurn my natural emotions
You make me feel I'm dirt and I'm hurt
And if I start a commotion
I run the risk of losing you and that's worse

Ever fallen in love with someone
Ever fallen in love -
        in love with someone
Ever fallen in love -
        in love with someone
You shouldn't've fallen in love with?

I can't see much of the future
Unless we find out what's to blame - what a shame
And we won't be together much longer
Unless we realise that we are the same

Ever fallen...

You disturb my natural emotions
You make me feel I'm dirt and I'm hurt
And if I start a commotion
I'll only end up losing you and that's worse

Ever fallen...

(c) Pete Shelly 1978 Virgin Music

Just Lust

There's bed in your eyes
But there's nothing there to trust
Just lust just lust
You're telling me lies
When you say that it's a must
Just lust just lust

You shattered all my dreams

You spurn my natural emotions
You make me feel I'm dirt and I'm hurt
And if I start a commotion
I run the risk of losing you and that's worse

Ever fallen in love with someone
Ever fallen in love, in love with someone
Ever fallen in love, in love with someone
You shouldn't have fallen in love with?

I can't see much of a future
Unless we find out what's to blame, what a shame
And we won't be together much longer
Unless we realize that we are the same

Ever fallen in love with someone
Ever fallen in love, in love with someone
Ever fallen in love, in love with someone
You shouldn't have fallen in love with

You disturb my natural emotions
You make me feel I'm dirt and I'm hurt
And if I start a commotion
I'll only end up losing you and that's worse

Ever fallen in love with someone
Ever fallen in love, in love with someone
Ever fallen in love, in love with someone
You shouldn't have fallen in love with?

Ever fallen in love with someone
Ever fallen in love, in love with someone
Ever fallen in love, in love with someone
You shouldn't have fallen in love with?

Ever fallen in love with someone
Ever fallen in love, in love with someone
Ever fallen in love, in love with someone
You shouldn't have fallen in love with?

Fallen in love with
Ever fallen in love with someone
You shouldn't have fallen in love with?

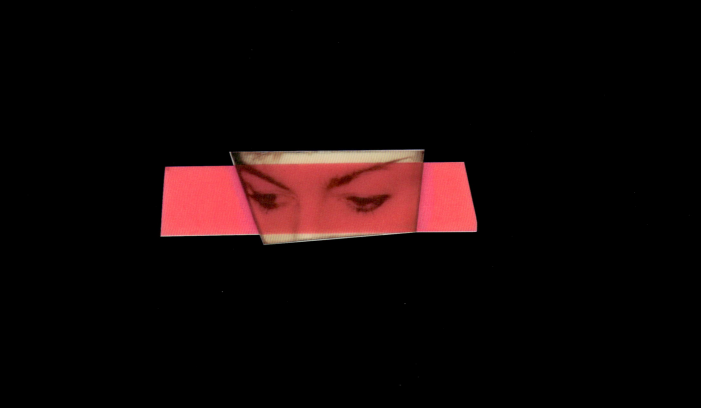

URSULA RODEL
THEMA
SELECTION
WEITE GASSE 9   0041
8001 ZÜRICH   TEL. 476626 / PRIV. 396405

SPERO MOLTO DA
RIVEDER TI !!
U.

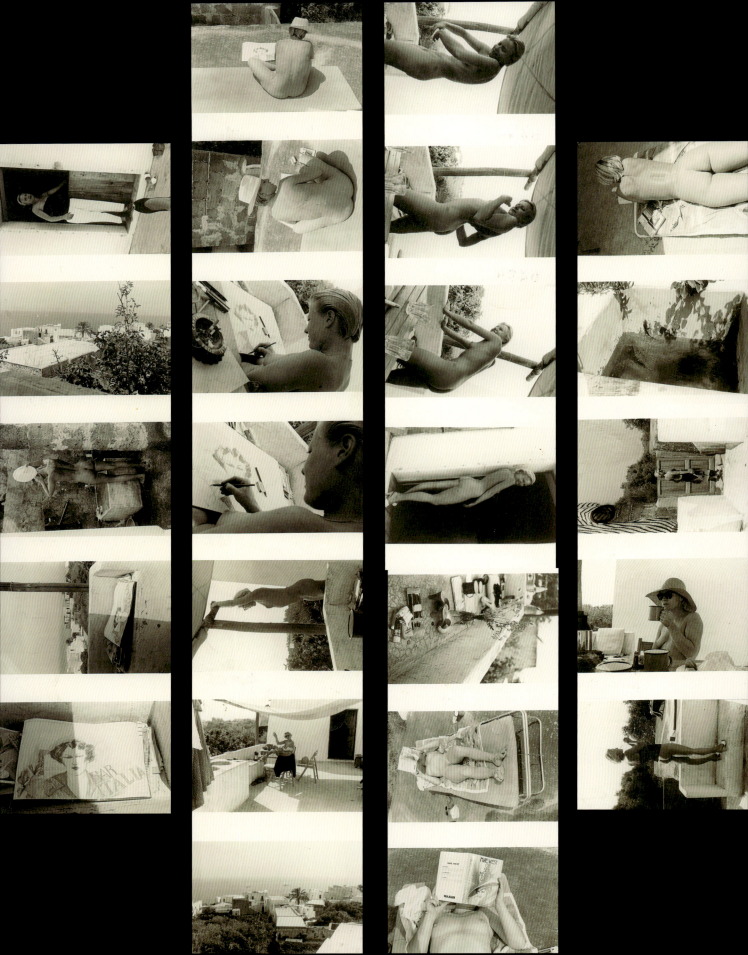

WOMEN ON THE MOVE
EFFECT
Stella Starr

27.5.78

12.8.78

23.5.78

12.8.78

12.8.78

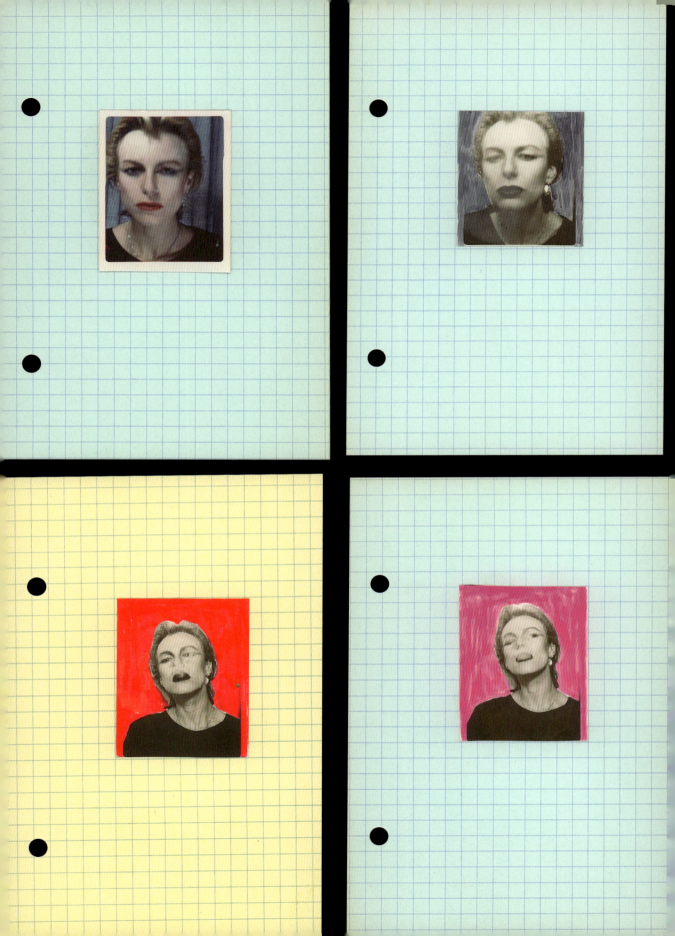

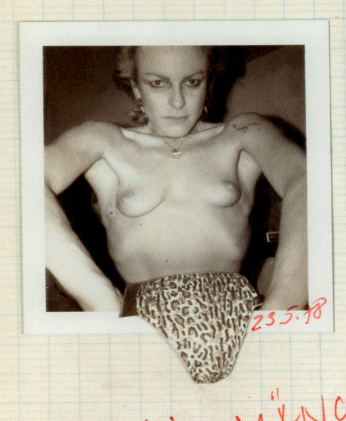

23.5.98

20 FIEV MÄNCHLEUS"
HORTON

A DREAM
by Andronica Cat

18.9.79.

d'affiche

FR3 «Rue Paul Colin» 21 H 30

16.7.24.

PLANUNG - THEMA

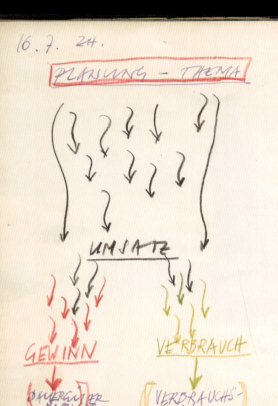

FUNKTIONEN

CHRISTA
VERKAUF, EV. SCHNITTE ?

ELISABETH
FABRIKATION — ~~FOTO~~
EV. ARBEIT VON SISSI
ZUTATEN

SISSI
VERKAUF PRESSE DOK.

URSULA
KOLLEKTION — STYLING

UTA
SCHNITTE KONTROLLIEREN,
ZUTATEN MUSTERZENTRALE, AUCH NEUE

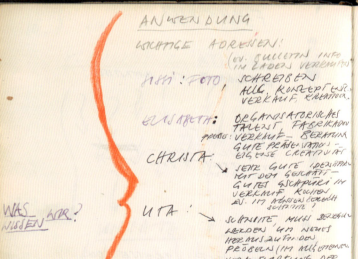

ANWENDUNG

WICHTIGE ADRESSEN:
(EV. BULLETIN INFO
IN ZADERS VERMITTL.)

SISSI: FOTO SCHREIBEN
ALLG. KONZEPT —
VERKAUF, KREATION.

ELISABETH: ORGANISATORISCHES
TALENT, FABRIKATION
FOTOS: VERKAUF — BERATUNG
GUTE PRÄSENTATION —
ERGEBNIS CREATIVITÄT

CHRISTA: SEHR GUTE IDENTIFIKATION
MIT DEM GESCHÄFT —
GUTES EINSPRING IM
VERKAUF KOCHEN
EV. IN GEWISSEN SACHEN
SCHNITTE ?

UTA: SCHNITTE, MUSS BEREIT
WERDEN UM NEUES
HERAUSZUFINDEN
PROBELN (IM ABLEHNEN)
VERANTWORTUNG DER
VERARBEITUNGSTECHNIK.

URSULA: ALLES WISSEN SEIN
MUSS — OHNE
KOMPROMISSE —
MUSS LERNEN BESSER
UEBERSICHT IM PLANEN
TERMINEN ect.

MUSS NICHT MEHR
FÜR JEDE KLEINIGKEIT ed.
INITIATIVE ERGREIFEN,
SHOW ect.
GETRAUT MICH SCHON NICHT
MEHR, KANN MIR VOR ect ect

WAS_WAR?
WISSEN WIR?

RATIONALISIEREN

VORTEILE

TELEFON
LICHT
PAPIER (VERWENDUNG
  VON NEUTRALEN
  ZETTEL —

ALLE: ALLG. SPESEN —

PROTOTYP + ZUTATEN
BESSER KALKULIEREN!
ZUTATEN VERBRAUCH:
STOFF EINKAUF?
LAGER MIT SACHEN DIE
UEBERALL HERUMLIEGEN?

BESSERE ORGANISATION
+ ARBEITSEINTEILUNG

- OBERES ZIMMER WIRD ZU
  BÜRO-DOKUMENTATIONSE.

NACHTEILE

EV. MEHR KORRESPONDENZ
(AUSLAND).

MEHR DISZIPLIN —

WIE SENKEN WIR
DIE KOSTEN

PARIS
GATO BARBIERI 3.12.79
PALACE

6.12.79
FILM: CLAUDE BERRY
AVEC CATHERINE DENEUVE

DREHEN: ENDE JANUAR 80
1. SCENE (WINTER)
MAI — CA 10 WOCHEN REST.
KLASKA MANTEL 7/8 FORM

~~MÄNTEL~~
KLEIDER MACHEN
IST KEINE KUNST
ICH GLAUBE DASS KLEIDER
SO WICHTIG SIND WIE
ESSEN LIEBEN ARBEIT
UND VERGNÜGEN

12-8-78

21.9.79

EDWIGE'S VISIT TO ZÜRICH

6.11.78

6.11.78

6.11.78

MARDI 7 NOV

Hello love,

I wish you good talking at the interview, not saying bad things — I think of you — see you soon — I like you lots. Up to nice cinema big kiss y.

Sats yets

le mariage c'est quelquechose d'
affreux.
je pense = moi

8.10.
A GOOD FRIEND
IS MORE THEN
10000 OF LOVERS...
OR BOTH IN ONE...

MONSTRUOS *** 15.5.78

16.5.78

SRG 20.20

Der junge Schweizer Filmregisseur Daniel Schmid.

Das Monatsmagazin

Die Uraufführung von Daniel Schmids neuestem Film «Violanta» an den Solothurner Filmtagen hat Andreas Vetsch zum Anlass genommen, den Davoser Filmkünstler zu porträtieren. Mit «Heute nacht oder nie», seinem ersten im Kino gezeigten Film, verschaffte Schmid sich grosse Aufmerksamkeit. Sein vorletztes Werk, «Der Schatten der Engel», das heftige Diskussionen um Form und Inhalt auslöste, brachte ihm auch internationale Anerkennung.

19.10.78

19.10.78

D

27.5.78

27.5.78

CALLAS FURIOSO —

MACHT GEIL UND…… NASS!!

27.5.78

27.5.78

ICH GLAUBE I MACH
MER GRAD NO
ES "SCHNÖIZLI"!

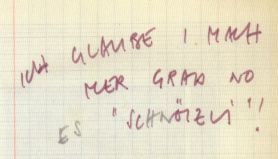
27.5.78

19.10.78

19.10.78

19.10.78

XXVI.X.78

XXVI.X.78

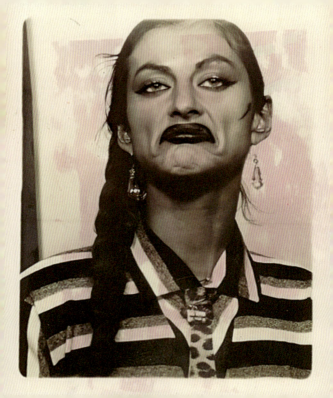

19.10.78

BAMOLA SPETTARE VOLARE...

Gummimantel ockerfarbig mit Goldschnur 77

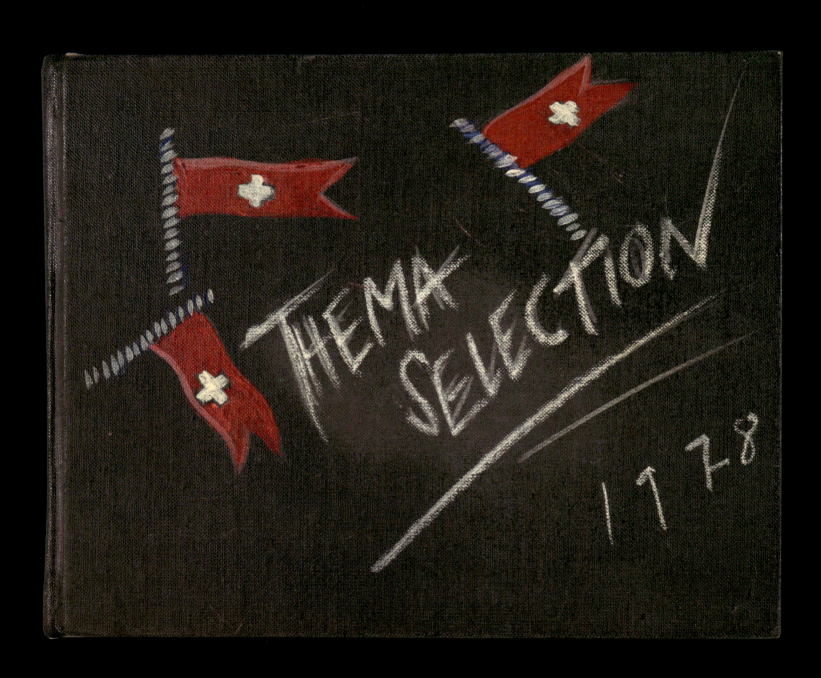

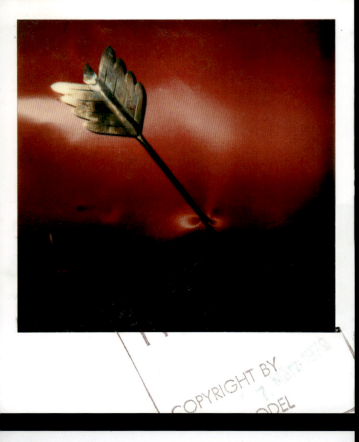

SATIN BIKINI '84

Jude porte-feuille
veste croisée en soie glacé
1976

I remember and kiss you!

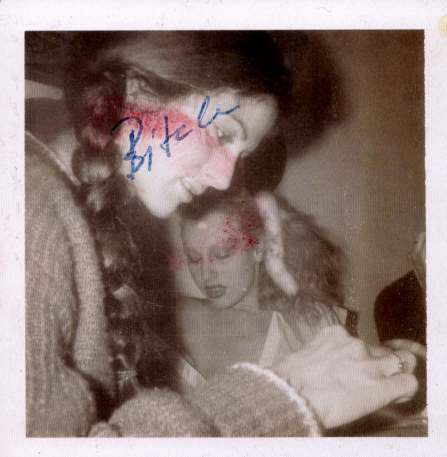

Schoffelgasse
28.4.80

Ich Wünsche
Dir Alles
Was DU
Brauchst

Love
Janet

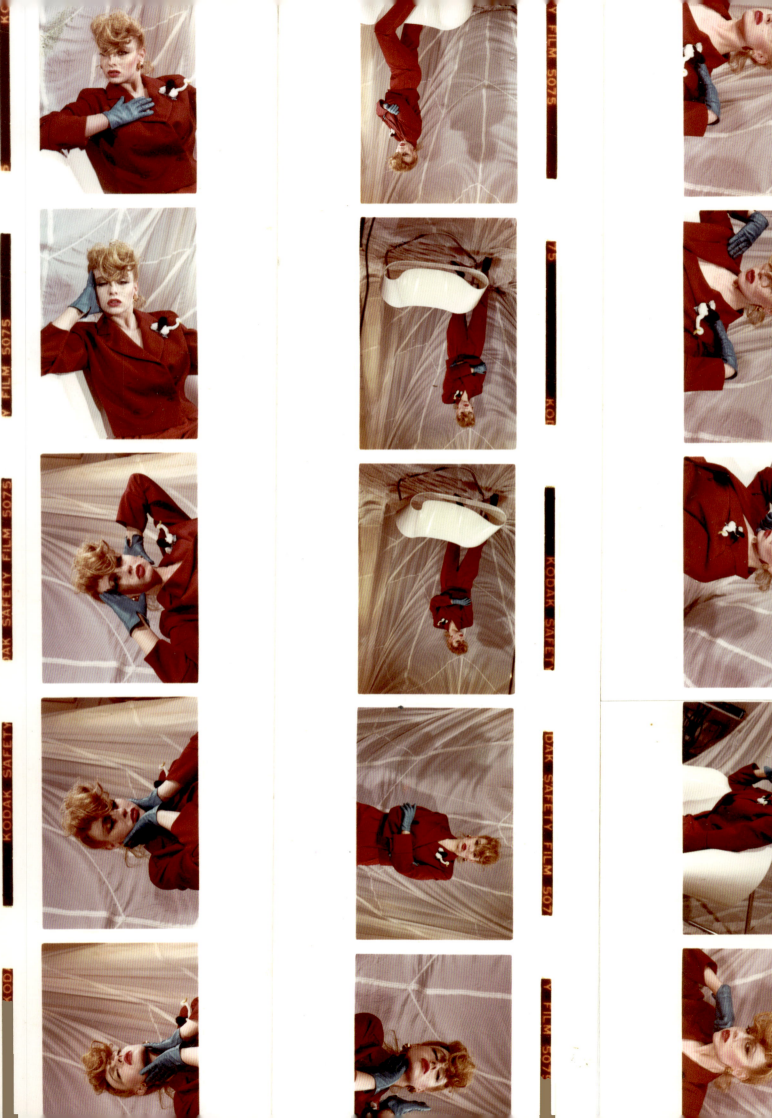

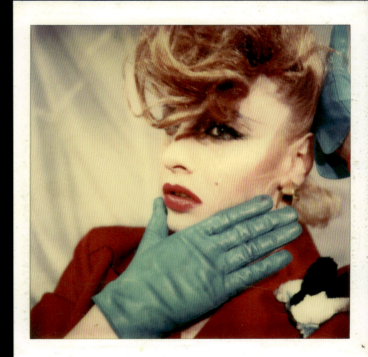

19. Juni 1979

POPELINE KLEID PYJAMAS (HERRENHEMD) 78

DOPPELREIHER ANZUG AUS WOLLTUCH 78

RUBBER COAT 78

LEDER JUPE 1980

ROBE DE CHAMBRE 1978

KLEID ENG, TIEFES DECOLLETÉ AUS SEIDEN- COUTURE

2-3-4-5 Maggio '79

IDEACOMO — Agnona
Tessuti a navetta e a maglia per mantelli, tailleurs, abiti da donna, uniti, stampati e operati in seta, lana e lino, e misti solo di fibre naturali.
Woven and knitted fabrics for overcoats, ladies suits and dresses, plain dyed, printed and jacquard in silk, wool and linen, mixed fabrics only in natural fibres.

è uscito il libro delle vacanze

18—16.5.79

Capri Capri

IDEACOMO — Albatex
Tessuti a navetta e a maglia per abiti da donna e camiceria, uniti e stampati, in seta, lana, cotone e fibre sintetiche.
Woven and knitted fabrics for ladies dresses and blouses plain dyed and printed on silk, wool, cotton and synthetic fibres.

IDEACOMO — Comoseta
Tessuti a navetta per abiti da donna e camiceria, stampati e uniti, in seta, lana, cotone, lino, fibre sintetiche e misti.
Woven fabrics for ladies dresses and blouses, printed and plain dyed on silk, wool, cotton, linen, mixed and synthetic fibres.

IDEACOMO — Braghenti
Tessuti a navetta per abiti da donna, camiceria e abbigliamento da mare, uniti, stampati e operati, in seta, lana, cotone, lino, fibre sintetiche e misti.
Woven fabrics for ladies dresses, blouses, shirts and beachwear, plain dyed, printed and jacquard in silk, wool, cotton, linen, mixed and synthetic fibres.

IDEACOMO — Bernasconi
Tessuti a navetta e a maglia per abiti da donna e camiceria, uniti, stampati e operati in lana, cotone, fibre sintetiche e misti.
Woven and knitted fabrics for ladies dresses and blouses, plain dyed, printed and jacquard in wool, cotton, linen, mixed and synthetic fibres.

NON TROPPO ALTA IL CAPO MOLTO BASSA!

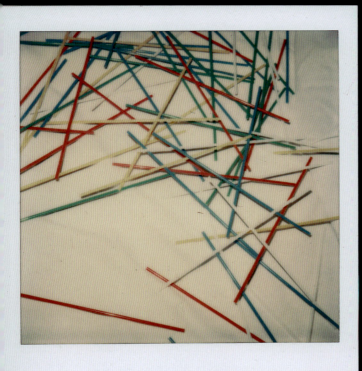

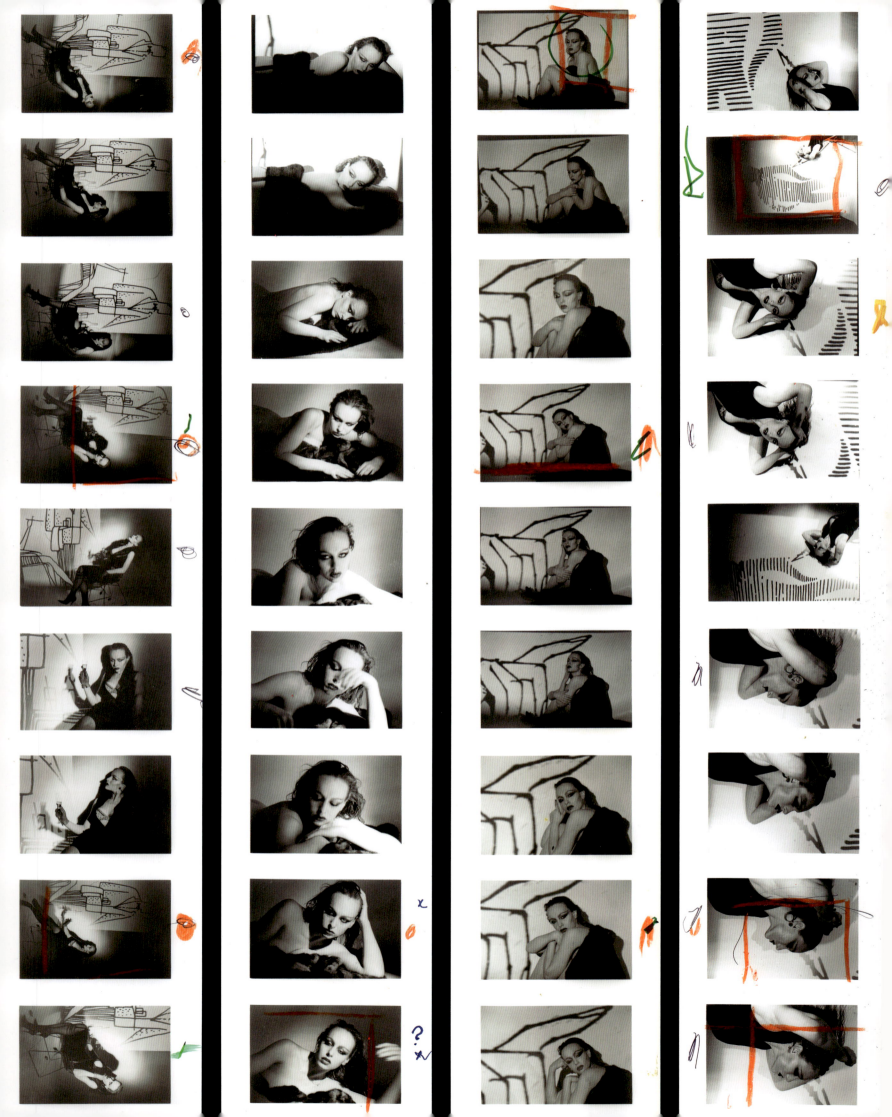

personalien

Irene Staub, 25, wurde in Zwinglis braver Stadt Zürich gesellschaftsfähig, nachdem sie vor Auserwählten des Schweizer Jet-Sets kostbare Abendroben vorgeführt hatte: Sie posierte als Mannequin auf dem Laufsteg der „Villa Egli". Beim anschließenden gemeinsamen Umtrunk stieß die Blondine, Champagner im Glas, mit den Damen aus der feinen Gesellschaft an. Nach der Darbietung aber verließ Irene Staub eilig die Villa, um ihren gewohnten Nachtdienst aufzunehmen: Als „Lady Shiva" ist sie nämlich Nummer eins unter den Straßenmädchen von Zürich („Ich mach' alles, auch mit Peitsche"). Irene, die auf eigenes Risiko und ohne Beschützer arbeitet, hat sich den besten Standplatz erobert und spricht am Rüdenplatz an der Limmat mögliche Kunden an: „Ich bekomme pro Leistung mindestens eine dreistellige Summe." Nach dem Erfolg bei der Modenschau wurde Irene Staub

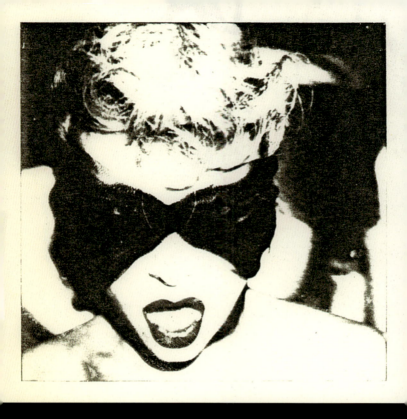

T-SHIRT 1980

RENN PRODUCTIONS

S.A.R.L. AU CAPITAL DE 300.000 F.

10, RUE LINCOLN - 75008 PARIS

TÉL. 256-25-90 + 359-82-15

Paris, le 27 Novembre 1980

Claude BERRI a le plaisir de vous inviter à la projection de son film :

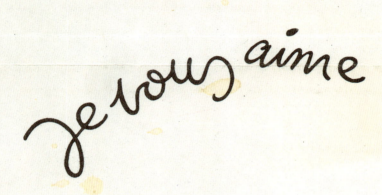

destinée aux acteurs, techniciens et amis et qui aura lieu le :

JEUDI 18 DECEMBRE 1980 à 20 h 30

au CLUB 13, 15 Avenue Hoche, 75008 Paris

En espérant vous y voir.

Invitation valable pour deux personnes.

Merci de confirmer votre présence en téléphonant à Janou Shammas :
359 82 15
ou 256 25 90

J.L. TRINTIGNANT
C. DENEUVE
G. DEPARDIEU
S. GAINSBOURG 82

FILM: "JE VOUS AIME"
COSTUME: J. RIDEL 82
TRINTIGNANT, DEPARDIEU, GAINSBOURG

C. DENEUVE, DEPARDIEU,
GAINSBOURG, TRINTIGNANT
SOUCHON   COSTUME: JE VOUS M...

C. DENEUVE
JACKE: MATELASSÉ SEIDE
FILM: "JE VOUS AIME"

CATHERINE GAINSBOURG DEPARDIEU

les fleurs de

DE PARIS

3, RUE DE DURAS, 75008 PARIS ∗ TÉLÉPHONE : (1) 266.00.28

C. DENEUVE +
J.L. TRINTIGNANT
(ILE MAURICE) 82

MMH....... BAND LEADER DEPROVEN!

VESTON CASHMERE
JE VOUS AIME 1980

SERGE GAINSBOURG
7.7.80

POP GROUPPE "BIJOUX"
DUREAU'S: DO YOU KNOW THEM?

C. DENEUVE, J.L. TRINTIGIS
FILM: "JE VOUS AIME." 82
ENGES SATINKLEID, SCHLANGENPR

N° 1

FERIEN
IN TUNIS
MIT CATHERINE

OKT. 78

GEB. 22.okt.

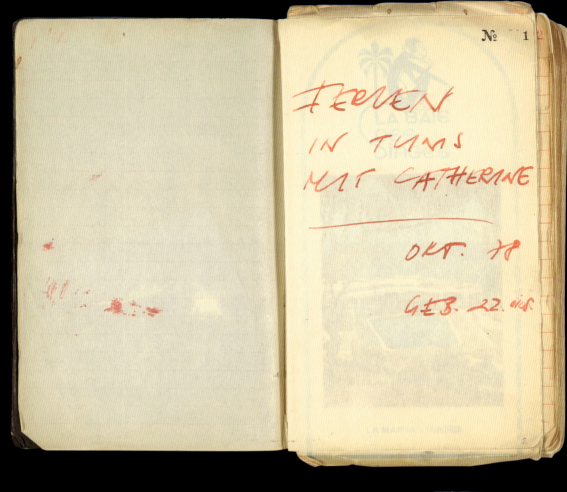

LA MARSA - TUNISIE

C D BREVAL 1.8.87

Monday 6h30

Good morning,
good day,
good break,
You were right to take it & I'm glad you're here and with me forever.
Love
Catherine

EVER FALLEN
IN LOVE

«ICH KONZENTRIERE MICH AUF DAS,
WAS MICH ZUTIEFST BEFRIEDIGT.»

Ursula Rodel

CHRISTINA SONDEREGGER

London sei ihre grosse Zeit gewesen, sagt Ursula Rodel. Vom ländlichen Meisterschwanden am Hallwilersee geht sie 1968 nach London ans College of Fashion. Alles ist neu und anders als das, was sie bis dahin gekannt hat. Sie belegt so viele Fächer, wie nur möglich; saugt alles auf und weiss, dass sie Mode machen will. Mit dem Diplom als Modezeichnerin kommt sie zurück in die Schweiz.

Als Jugendliche habe sie lange nicht gewusst, was sie werden wollte. Die Eltern führten ein nobles Hotel und Ursula fand, sie habe die schönste Mutter: gepflegt, elegant und immer mit rotem Lippenstift und rot lackierten Nägeln. Ihre Mutter habe ihr Frauenbild stark geprägt, stellt sie mit einer gewissen Distanz zu ihrer Kindheit fest. Ursula Rodel hat nie versucht, jemanden zu kopieren, sondern hat sich als Kind schon ihre eigene Garderobe zugelegt: Eine Windjacke, Skihosen, die sie bis zu den Knien hochzog, so dass es aussah, als wären es Knickerbocker. Dazu trug sie dicke, gestrickte Socken in offenen Ledersandalen, die knirschten, wenn sie über Kies lief. Es waren Bubenkleider, die sie für sich aussuchte. Heimlich und nur für sich hat sie diese Stücke getragen.

«ICH FAND MICH SCHÖN UND FÜHLTE MICH ZUM ERSTEN MAL WOHL IN MEINEN KLEIDERN. DAS WAR DER KERN MEINER SPÄTEREN ERKENNTNIS.»

Ursula Rodel

Während ihrer Ausbildung in London und einer dreimonatigen Reise quer durch die USA wird ihr klar, dass sie ihre eigenen Kleider machen will. Doch so schnell ging es nicht. Als Einkäuferin und Stylistin in einem grossen Zürcher Warenhaus lernt sie wichtige Leute kennen und erhält die Möglichkeit, geschäftlich zu reisen. Ihre Arbeitskollegin, Katharina Bébié-Lardelli (1939), und sie machen sich bald schon selbständig und gründen einen eigenen Styling-Service. Aber Beratung ist nicht gleichbedeutend mit Selbermachen und so setzt Ursula Rodel alles daran, einen Laden für ihre Modekollektion, die sie bereits im Kopf hat, zu finden und nach ihrem Stil einzurichten.

1972 eröffnet sie zusammen mit Sissi Zöbeli (1949) und Katharina Bébié-Lardelli ihren Laden *Thema Selection* mit dem gleichnamigen Prêt-à-Porter Label. Noch muss sie auf den Erfolg warten. Die Leute zögern. Ursula Rodel entwirft für die selbstbewusste, berufstätige Frau. Der Stil ist avantgardistisch, reduziert, androgyn.

«IN DEN 70ER-JAHREN GAB ES NOCH KEINE JUNGE MODE IN ZÜRICH. WIR WAREN PIONIERINNEN UND URSULA RODEL WAR DIE ERSTE, DIE EINE WIRKLICH EIGENSTÄNDIGE KOLLEKTION GEMACHT HAT.»

Ruth Grüninger, Modedesignerin und Mitbegründerin des Labels *Pink Flamingo*, 2023

Die 70er-Jahre müssen sich für Rodel wie ein Zeitraffer angefühlt haben. Alles geschieht gleichzeitig, alles verändert sich. Auch sie verändert sich. Die blonden Locken weichen einem Kurzhaarschnitt, den sie in einen gestylten New Wave-Look nach hinten kämmt. Die Augen und Brauen sind katzenhaft betont. Ihr Ausdruck ist androgyn. Mitte der 70er-Jahre beginnt Rodel ausgiebig zu fotografieren: Sich selbst, ihre Mode, ihre Musen, ihre Freundinnen und Freunde, Ferien, Filmsets und Prominente. Die Bilder halten fest, was in grossem Tempo und an immer neuen Schauplätzen geschieht. Das Prinzip des Sofortbildes kommt ihr entgegen. Kein langes Warten auf die Entwicklung, sondern unmittelbares Betrachten des Resultats. Diese Geschwindigkeit entspricht der Schnelligkeit ihres Lebenswandels. Ihre Mode indessen ist alles andere als schnelllebig. Zwar ist auch sie dem Diktat der wechselnden Kollektionen unterworfen, aber ihr Stil bleibt zeitlos, die Qualität unverändert hochwertig.

Einige ihrer Fotos datiert Ursula Rodel. Manche versieht sie mit Bemerkungen, andere mit ausführlichen Legenden. Ein paar bearbeitet sie mit Stift oder Farbe. Es handelt sich dabei um spontane, humorvolle oder korrigierende Eingriffe, nicht zu verwechseln mit einem bewussten, künstlerischen Akt. Dass Ursula Rodel die Fotos bearbeitet ist typisch für sie, denn sie verleiht allem, was sie anfasst, ihren persönlichen Stil.

«HINTER IHREM PERFEKT GESTYLTEN AUFTRETEN VERBARG SICH EIGENTLICH EINE SEHR SCHEUE PERSON.»

Sissi Zöbeli, Geschäftsinhaberin von *Thema Selection* und Entwerferin, 2023

Das häufigste Sujet ist ihr Gesicht. Sie fotografiert sich in ganzen Serien, die sich nur durch Nuancen in der Kopfhaltung, im Blick oder im Ausdruck voneinander unterscheiden. Oft suchen ihre Augen den Fokus. Der Blick ist direkt, beinahe provozierend.

Die weit vorgestreckte Hand mit der Kamera ist noch sichtbar. Auf anderen Selbstporträts meidet sie den direkten Augenkontakt mit der Kamera. Sie wendet sich scheu ab, als wolle sie sich gar nicht fotografieren. Ein andermal kokettiert sie mit Accessoires: Sonnenbrillen, Kopfbedeckungen oder auch die Zigarette im Mundwinkel verleihen ihr einen verwegenen Ausdruck. Mit ihren Polaroidbildern offenbart sie zahlreiche Facetten ihrer Persönlichkeit. Sie ist nicht eine, sie ist viele. Provokativ, scheu oder maskiert. Wie Zorro, der immer eine Maske trägt und den Ursula Rodel in einem ihrer frühen Erinnerungsbüchlein allen ihren Selbstporträts voranstellt. Sie selbst hat sich nie zu ihren Bildern geäussert. Die grosse Menge in ihrem Nachlass lässt aber darauf schliessen, dass ihr das Fotografieren wichtig war.

«URSULA WAR IMMER NEUGIERIG AUF ALLE ZEITSTRÖMUNGEN.»

This Brunner, Kurator für Filmkunst, 2023

In den 70er-Jahren ist die Sofortbildkamera ein neues künstlerisches Instrument sowie ein beliebtes Mittel zur Selbstdarstellung und Dokumentation. Es braucht kein technisches Know-How und vieles bleibt dem Zufall überlassen. Ursula Rodel bringt es auf dem Umschlag ihres Erinnerungsbüchleins LIFE LIFE auf den Punkt: «*Simply press one button. Nothing to focus or set. Motor ejects the picture. It develops in minutes.*» Andy Warhol (1928–1987), den Rodel in New York kennenlernt, fotografiert damit seine Sammlerinnen und Sammler. Er selbst lässt sich mit der Polaroidkamera portraitieren. Auch David Hockney (1937) setzt die Polaroidkamera als künstlerisches Mittel ein, sei es zur Definierung eines Motivs, oder zum Festhalten von Schnappschüssen. Eine Vorreiterin für die Polaroidfotografie in der Schweiz ist die Bildhauerin Hannah Villiger (1951–1997). In den 80er-Jahren wird sie mit ihren grossformatigen Fotografien berühmt. Die Künstlerin fotografiert zumeist ihren eigenen Körper, tastet ihn mit der Polaroidkamera ab und schafft fragmentierte, teils abstrakte Körperbilder. Die Kamera ist maximal eine Armlänge entfernt, wie bei Ursula Rodel. Rodel geht nicht mit der selben Stringenz vor wie Villiger, sondern weitet die Bandbreite ihrer Sujets auf ihre Musen und ihre Mode aus. Die Fotografie bleibt Nebenbeschäftigung und Dokumentationsmittel, während die Mode die erste Rolle spielt. Am Rande kann man Rodel in eine Tendenz einreihen, in der Künstlerinnen sich das Selbstporträt zu Eigen machen und damit in ein bis anhin mehrheitlich von Männern besetztes Genre eindringen.

In verschiedenen Erinnerungsbüchern hält Ursula Rodel ihre Ferien und Reisen fest. Es ist immer wieder der gleiche Freundeskreis in wechselnder Zusammensetzung, sei es 1975 am Strand von Cannes, in New York oder Portofino, auf Mykonos, Pantelleria oder auf Stromboli. Die Bücher zeugen von unbeschwertem Nichtstun, Ausgelassenheit, von Nähe und viel nackter Haut.

«WIR WAREN EINE IDEALE REISEGRUPPE. URSULA RODEL WAR DABEI, ELISABETH BOSSARD SOWIESO, RUEDI HAENE, THOMAS AMMANN UND IRENE STAUB, ALIAS LADY SHIVA. WIR HATTEN TOTAL WILDE ZEITEN.»

This Brunner, 2023

Liebesbeziehungen kommen und gehen oder laufen parallel. Ursula Rodel lebt ihr Lesbischsein intensiv aus. In ihren Kreisen wird kein Aufheben darum gemacht, wer mit wem eine sexuelle Beziehung pflegt, sei sie gleichgeschlechtlich oder heterosexuell. Die Zeit ist hybrid, vieles ist möglich. Ursula Rodel legt Erinnerungsbücher mit intimen Fotos und Liebesschwüren an. Der Songtext «Ever Fallen in Love» der Band Buzzcocks findet sich auch darin: Enttäuschung und Leidenschaft liegen nahe beieinander. Dennoch ist jede neue Liebe ein neuer Kick.

«EROTICISM SENSUALITY TENDERNESS SEXUALITY… ALL TOGETHER IS LOVE»

Ursula Rodel, 1981

Um 1978 begegnet Ursula Rodel Catherine Deneuve. Eine langjährige Freundschaft nimmt ihren Anfang. Ursula Rodel ist für die Filmgarderobe von Catherine Deneuve in mehreren Filmen zuständig und begleitet sie an die Drehorte oder sie verbringt ihre Ferien gemeinsam mit ihr. Auch jetzt fotografiert Rodel. Die Polaroidkamera geht durch viele Hände und so ist auch sie auf einigen Schnappschüssen zu sehen, sei es mit Catherine Deneuve, Serge Gainsbourg oder mit Gérard Depardieu. Die Overalls, die die Musiker der Punk-Band Bijou mit Frontsänger Depardieu im Film «Je vous aime» (1980) tragen, stammen ebenfalls von Ursula Rodel. Rodel lebt zirka ein Jahr in Paris. Dort lernt sie auch Edwige Belmore kennen. Die «Queen of Punk» ist eng mit dem Fotografen Pierre Commoy (Pierre et Gilles) befreundet und Ursula bittet

Pierre, sie zu fotografieren – das ikonische Bild von ihr als Punk, auf den ersten Seiten dieses Buches, entsteht.

> *«URSULA HÄTTE NACH PARIS ODER LONDON GEHEN SOLLEN. SIE WAR EIN SUPERTALENT UND DIE SCHWEIZ KEIN MODELAND.»*
>
> Sissi Zöbeli, 2023

Irene Staub war Ursula Rodels grosse Muse, ihre wichtigste Inspirationsquelle. Dieser Körper und diese erotische Ausstrahlung war einmalig. So eine Frau gab es kein zweites Mal, erinnert sich Ursula Rodel. Als Prostituierte war Irene hochprofessionell, als Privatperson hingegen fehlte ihr das nötige Selbstbewusstsein. Ursula hat sie überall hin mitgenommen, nach New York, Rom, Paris und hat sie wichtigen Leuten vorgestellt. Ihr tragischer Tod 1989 trifft Ursula Rodel sehr schmerzhaft. Auch wenn sie andere Musen und Freundinnen gehabt hat, über allen stand Irene.

> *«MIT IHRER MODE GAB URSULA RODEL DER FRAU EIN MITTEL, ATTRAKTIV ZU SEIN UND JEMANDEN VERFÜHREN ZU KÖNNEN. MIT DIESER ART VON «POP-FEMINISMUS», WIE ER HEUTE VON EINER JÜNGEREN GENERATION GELEBT WIRD, GEHÖRTE SIE DAMALS ZUR AVANTGARDE.»*
>
> Bice Curiger, Kunsthistorikerin und Kuratorin, 2023

Der Nachlass von Ursula Rodel, den das Schweizerische Nationalmuseum 2021 in seine Sammlung aufnehmen konnte, ist reich an Fotos, Erinnerungsbüchern, Kollektionszeichnungen, Skizzen, Kunst und Kleidern. In seiner Gesamtheit bildet der Bestand das Leben einer aussergewöhnlichen, kämpferischen Frau in einer bewegten Zeit ab und dokumentiert das Schaffen einer Schweizer Modeschöpferin der ersten Stunde. Ohne am politisch-feministischen Diskurs aktiv teilzunehmen, hat sie mit ihren Modeentwürfen zur Emanzipation der Frau beigetragen, indem sie ihr ein Instrumentarium in die Hand gegeben hat, ihre Persönlichkeit als selbstbewusste, unabhängige, moderne Frau auszudrücken. Für das Schweizerische Nationalmuseum ist Ursula Rodels Werk ein wichtiges Zeugnis eines pionierhaften, kreativen Frauenlebens.

EVER FALLEN
IN LOVE

«I FOCUS ON WHAT DEEPLY SATISFIES ME.»

Ursula Rodel

CHRISTINA SONDEREGGER

According to Ursula Rodel, London was her big time. She moved from rural Meisterschwanden on Lake Hallwil in Switzerland to attend the London *College of Fashion* in 1968. Compared to what she had previously known, everything there was new and unusual. She enrolled in as many classes as she could, learned as much as possible and in the end, was determined to design garments; returning to Switzerland with a degree in fashion illustrator.

She struggled with deciding what she wanted to do with her life as a youngster. Her parents ran a fancy hotel. Ursula believed she had the most beautiful mother since she was always elegant, well-groomed, and wore red lipstick and painted nails. She acknowledges, looking back at her youth, that her mother had a significant impact on her perception of women. But Ursula Rodel never tried to imitate anyone; instead, she acquired her own outfits as a child: a windbreaker and ski pants that she pulled up to her knees to resemble knickerbockers. With them, she wore thick, knitted socks and open-toed leather sandals that crunched when she walked over gravel. They were boys' dresses, that she chose for herself and wore these pieces secretly.

> «I FOUND MYSELF BEAUTIFUL
> AND FELT COMFORTABLE IN MY CLOTHES
> FOR THE FIRST TIME. THAT WAS AT THE CORE
> OF MY LATER REALIZATION.»
>
> Ursula Rodel

She discovered her passion for fashion during her time in London and a three-month journey across the United States. But it took a while to happen. While working as a buyer and stylist at a sizable department store in Zürich, she meets influential people and has the chance to travel for business. She quickly establishes her own styling service with coworker Katharina Bébié-Lardelli (1939). However, consulting is not the same as producing fashion, so Ursula Rodel looks for the appropriate store to house the range of clothes she has in her mind and styled the place accordingly.

Together with Sissi Zöbeli (1949) and Katharina Bébié-Lardelli, she establishes the Zürich-based prêt-à-porter label *Thema Selection* in 1972. Success takes time. People are hesitant. Ursula Rodel designs for the self-confident, professional woman. The style is avant-garde, reduced, androgynous.

> «IN THE 1970S, THERE WAS NO YOUNG
> FASHION IN ZÜRICH. WE WERE PIONEERS
> AND URSULA RODEL WAS THE FIRST TO MAKE
> A REALLY INDEPENDENT COLLECTION»
>
> Ruth Grüninger, fashion designer and co-founder
> of the *Pink Flamingo* label, 2023

For Rodel, the 1970s must have seemed to fly by. Everything changes constantly. She is also changing. The blonde curls get cut, she now dons a short haircut that she styles into a New Wave-inspired appearance, accentuated by exaggerated cat-like brows and eyes. She has an androgynous expression. Midway through the 1970s, Rodel starts taking a lot of photos of herself, her fashion, her muses, her friends, trips, movie sets, and famous people. The images document what is occurring in her orbit at the time. The principle of the instant picture suits her. No need to wait – you have the result in your hands right away, a pace that is consistent with her way of living. But her sense of style in fashion is anything but fast moving. Even if she too is governed by the rhythm of new collections, her style, and sense for high quality never go out of fashion.

Some of Ursula Rodel's photographs have noted dates. She adds remarks to some and lengthy bylines to others. She paints or uses a pen to modify a few. These are impromptu, comedic, or corrective interventions, not a deliberate, artistic performance. Since Ursula Rodel imbues everything she touches with her distinctive sense of style, the fact that she alters the images is a quintessential trademark of her.

> «BEHIND HER PERFECTLY STYLED
> APPEARANCE WAS ACTUALLY A VERY
> SHY PERSON.»
>
> Sissi Zöbeli, owner of *Thema Selection*
> and designer, 2023

The most frequent subject in her photography becomes her face. She develops complete series that are only marginally different from one another in terms of head posture, gaze, or expression. Frequently, she stares directly at the lens. Direct and almost confrontational, the look. Still discernible is the hand holding the camera that is extended far in front.

In other self-portraits, she avoids making direct eye contact with the camera. She turns away shyly, as if she doesn't want to be captured in photos at all. She sometimes plays with her accessories: sunglasses, headgear, or even a cigarette in the corner of her mouth lend her an audacious expression. With her Polaroid pictures, she reveals numerous facets of her personality. She is not one, she is many. Provocative, shy or masked. Like Zorro, who always wears a mask and whom Ursula Rodel prefixes to all her self-portraits in one of her early memory booklets. She herself never commented on her photographs. But the large number suggests that taking photos was important to her.

«URSULA WAS ALWAYS CURIOUS ABOUT ALL THE TRENDS OF THE TIME.»

This Brunner, Curator of Film Arts, 2023

In the 1970s the instant camera is a novel artistic instrument as well as a widely-liked tool for self-expression and recording. It is portable and doesn't call for any technological expertise. On the front of her memory booklet LIFE LIFE, Ursula Rodel sums it up: «*Simply press one button. Nothing to focus or set. Motor ejects the picture. It develops in minutes*». Andy Warhol (1928-1987), whom Rodel met in New York, used it to photograph his collectors. He himself had one of his portraits taken with the Polaroid camera. David Hockney (1937) also uses the Polaroid camera as an artistic tool, whether to define a subject or to capture snapshots. A pioneer of Polaroid photography in Switzerland is the sculptor Hannah Villiger (1951-1997). She became famous in the 1980s with her large-format photographs. The artist mostly photographs her own body, scans it with the Polaroid camera and creates fragmented, partly abstract body images. The camera is at most an arm's length away, as in Ursula Rodel's work. Rodel does not proceed with the same stringency as Villiger, but expands the range of her subjects to include her muses and her fashion. Photography remains a sideline and means of documentation, while fashion plays the primary role. On the margins, Rodel can be seen as part of a trend in which female artists are making self-portraiture their own, thus penetrating a genre hitherto predominantly occupied by men.

Ursula Rodel records her vacations and travels in various memory books. It's always the same circle of friends in a changing composition, whether it's 1975 on the beach in Cannes, in New York or Portofino, on Mykonos, Pantelleria or on Stromboli. The books bear witness to carefree idleness, exuberance, closeness, and lots of naked skin.

«WE WERE AN IDEAL TRAVEL GROUP. URSULA RODEL WAS THERE, ELISABETH BOSSARD ANYWAY, RUEDI HAENE, THOMAS AMMANN AND IRENE STAUB, ALIAS LADY SHIVA. WE HAD TOTALLY WILD TIMES.»

This Brunner, 2023

Affairs and relationships come and go or run parallel. Ursula Rodel lives out her lesbianism intensively. No fuss is made about who has a sexual relationship with whom, be it same-sex or heterosexual in her circles. The time is hybrid, many things are possible. Ursula Rodel creates memory booklets with intimate photos and love vows. The lyrics to the song «ever fallen in love» by the punk band Buzzcocks can also be found in them: disappointment and passion lie close together. Still, every new love is a new thrill.

«EROTICISM SENSUALITY TENDERNESS SEXUALITY... ALL TOGETHER IS LOVE»

Ursula Rodel, 1981

Catherine Deneuve and Ursula Rodel first cross paths in 1978, starting a long friendship. In various films, Ursula Rodel oversees Catherine Deneuve's wardrobe and travels with her to the shooting locations or on vacations. She can also be seen in some photos taken with Catherine Deneuve, Serge Gainsbourg, or Gérard Depardieu because the Polaroid camera changes hands frequently. Ursula Rodel also created the overalls worn by the band members of the punk group Bijou, which featured lead vocalist Gérard Depardieu, in the 1980 movie «Je vous aime». Rodel spent nearly a year residing in Paris. She meets Edwige Belmore there. The «Queen of Punk» is close friends with photographer Pierre Commoy (Pierre et Gilles), and Ursula asks Pierre to take her picture, which results in the famous punk portrait that appears on the first pages of this book.

> *«URSULA SHOULD HAVE GONE TO PARIS OR LONDON. SHE WAS A SUPER TALENT, AND SWITZERLAND WAS NOT A FASHION COUNTRY.»*
>
> Sissi Zöbeli, 2023

Ursula Rodel's greatest inspiration and muse was Irene Staub. Her sensual charisma and body were exceptional. There was no woman like her. Irene was a very skilled prostitute, but as a private person she lacked the required self-assurance. She traveled with Ursula to New York, Rome, and Paris, where she made introductions to influential people. Her tragic death in 1989 hit Ursula Rodel painfully. Even if she had other muses and friends, Irene stood above them all.

> *«WITH HER FASHION, URSULA RODEL GAVE WOMEN A MEANS OF BEING ATTRACTIVE AND BEING ABLE TO SEDUCE SOMEONE. WITH THIS KIND OF «POP FEMINISM» AS IT IS LIVED TODAY BY A YOUNGER GENERATION, SHE BELONGED TO THE AVANT-GARDE AT THAT TIME.»*
>
> Bice Curiger, art historian and curator, 2023

The Ursula Rodel estate is filled with photographs, memory booklets, collection drawings, sketches, art and clothing, all of which the Swiss National Museum was able to add to its collection in 2021. The complete inventory records the efforts of a pioneering Swiss fashion designer and portrays the life of an extraordinary, combative woman in a volatile era. She made a contribution to women's emancipation through her fashion creations, without actively participating in the political-feminist discourse. She gave women a set of tools to express their personalities as self-assured, independent, modern women. For the Swiss National Museum, the work of Ursula Rodel serves as a significant testament to a trailblazing, creative woman's life.

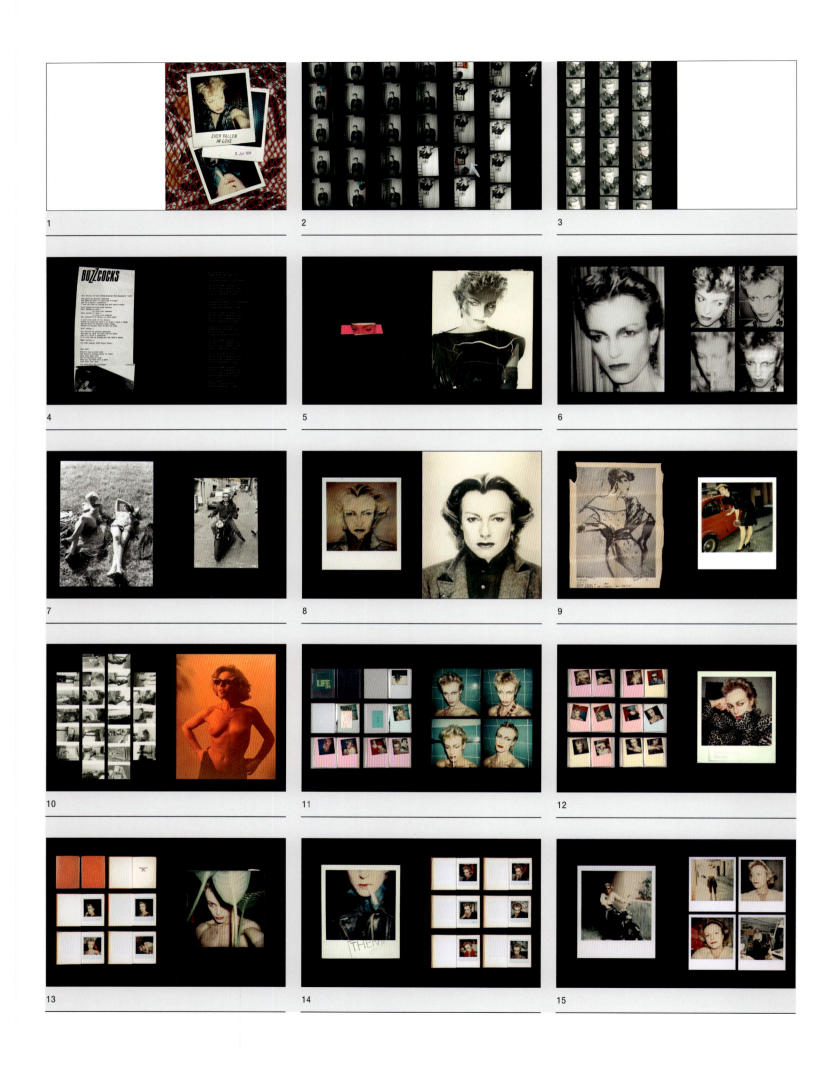

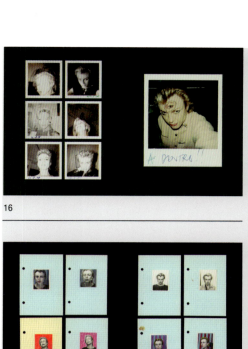

16

17

18

19

20

21

22

23

24

25

26

27

28

29

30

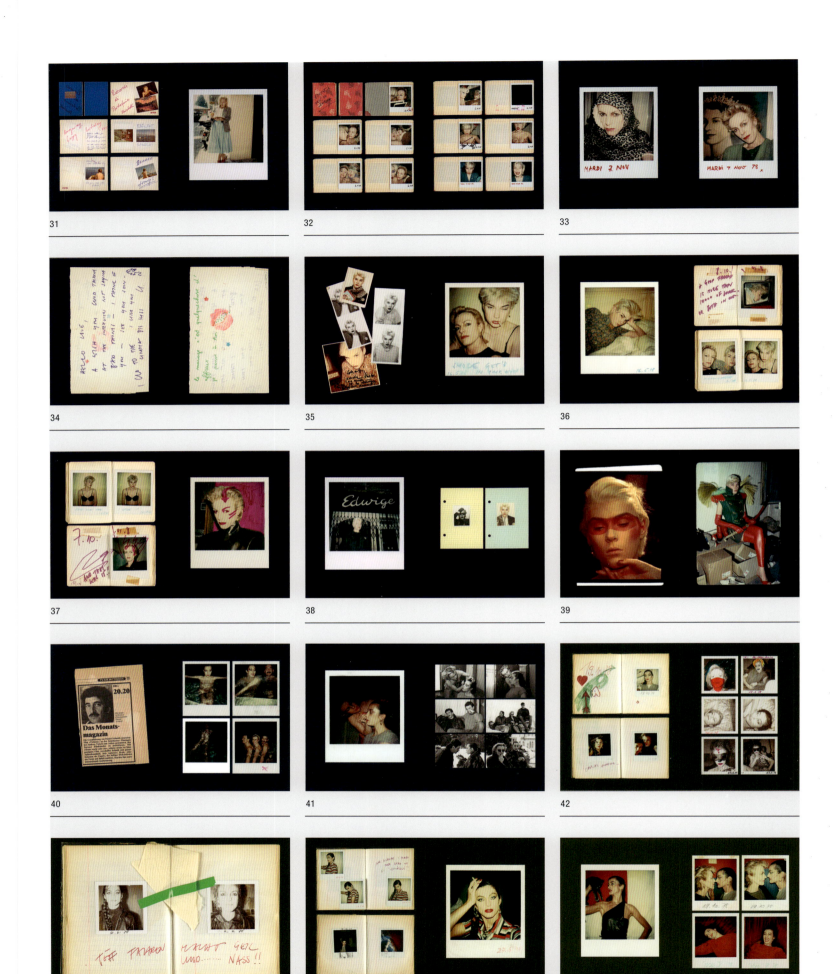

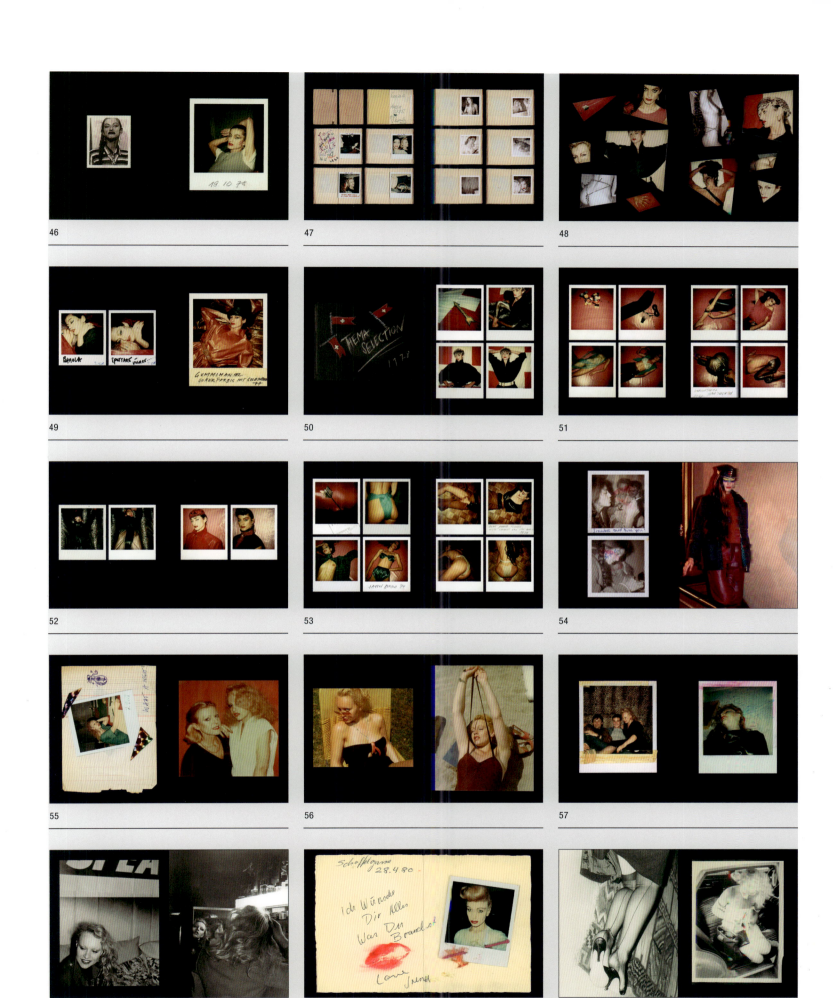

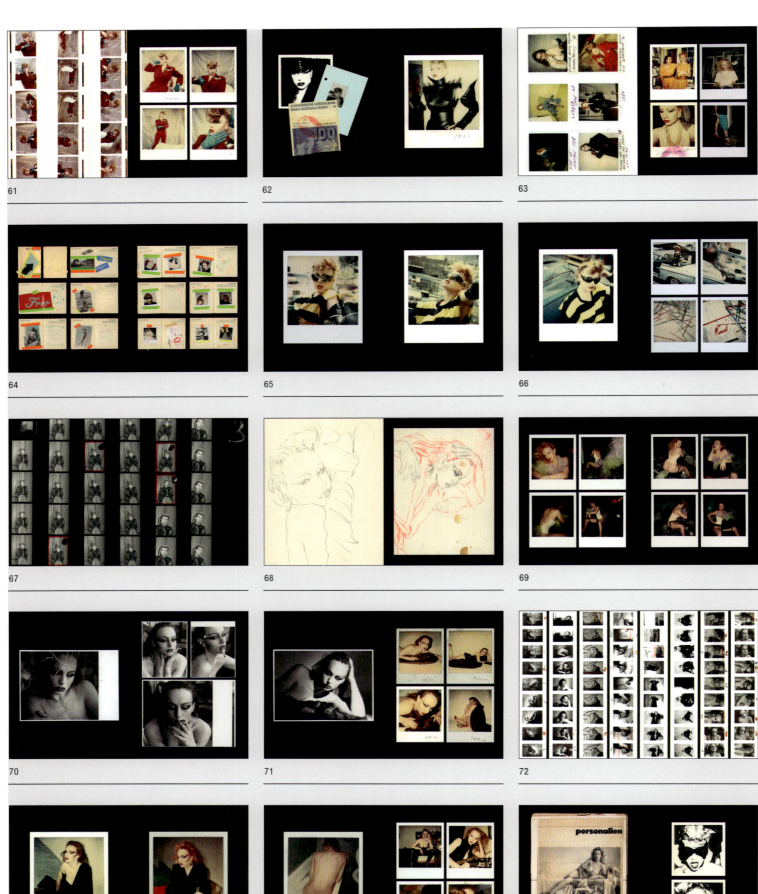

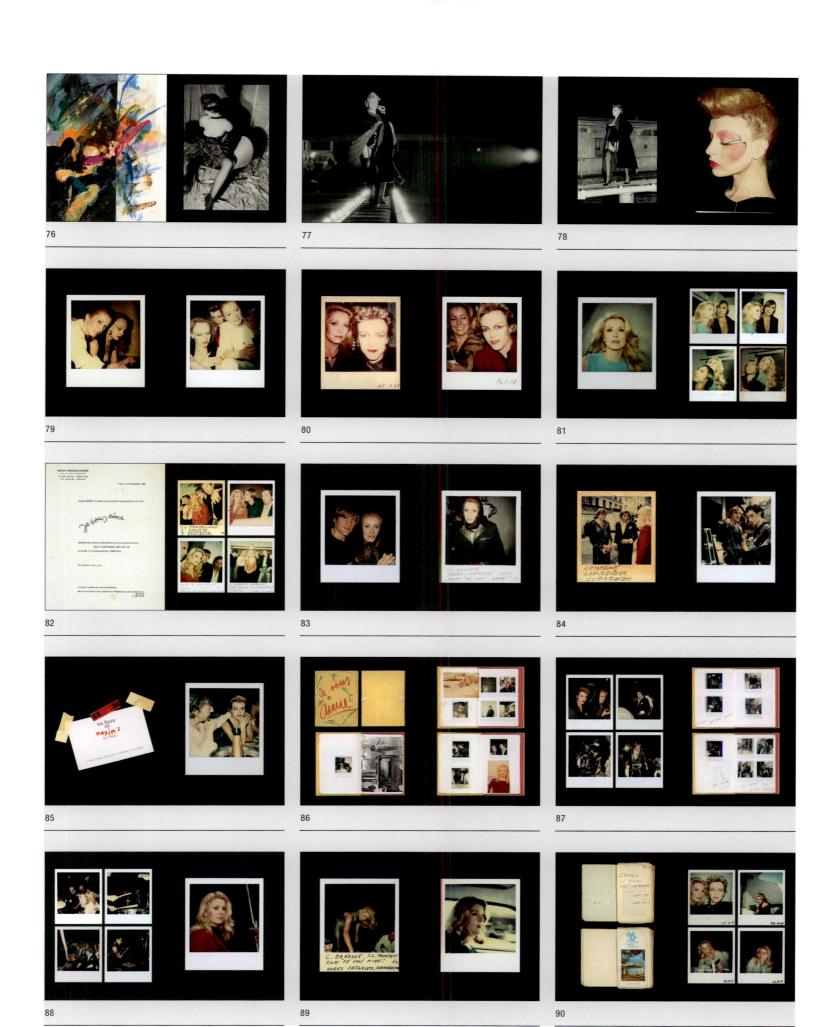

Rechte Seite: *(v. o. nach u.)* LM 185227.7 / LM 183725.2
LM 181819, GBE 163584 / LM 181820

1

Beide Seiten: LM 183721.2-36

2

Linke Seite: LM 183721.74-91

3

Linke Seite: LM 181840.1

4

Linke Seite: LM 181840.1, GBE 162999
Rechte Seite: LM 183751.1 © *PIERRE COMMOY*

5

Linke Seite: LM 183747.2
Rechte Seite: *(v. l. nach r. u. von o. nach u.)* LM 183726.3
LM 183746.2 / LM 183748.1 / LM 183746.1

6

Linke Seite: LM 183773
Rechte Seite: LM 183741.1

7

Linke Seite: LM 181827.6
Rechte Seite: LM 183750

8

Linke Seite: LM 181833, GBE 163727
Rechte Seite: LM 183727.5

9

Linke Seite: *(von l. nach r. u. pro Streifen)*
1. Streifen *(v. o. nach u.)* LM 185222.52 / LM 185222.17-21
2. Streifen *(v. o. nach u.)* LM 185222.3-6 / LM 185222.49-50
3. Streifen *(v. o. nach u.)* LM 185222.61 / LM 185222.60
LM 185222.59 / LM 185222.58 / LM 185222.31-32
4. Streifen *(v. o. nach u.)* LM 185222.42-43 / LM 185222.45-47
Rechte Seite: LM 181836.11

10

Linke Seite: *(v. l. nach r. u. v. o. nach u.)*
LM 181817 / LM 181817, GBE 163511 / LM 181817
GBE 163512 / LM 181817, GBE 163513 / LM 181817
GBE 163518 / LM 181817, GBE 163520
Rechte Seite: *(von l. nach r. u. von o. nach u.)*
LM 181817, GBE 163514 / LM 181817, GBE 163516
LM 181817, GBE 163515 / LM 181817, GBE 163515

11

Linke Seite: *(v. l. nach r. u. v. o. nach u.)*
LM 181817 / GBE 163522 / LM 181817, GBE 163523
LM 181817, GBE 163529 / LM 181817, GBE 163530
LM 181817, GBE 163527 / LM 181817, GBE 163524
Rechte Seite: LM 181817, GBE 163521

12

Linke Seite: *(v. l. nach r. u. v. o. nach u.)*
LM 181819 / LM 181819, GBE 163548 / LM 181819
GBE 163550 / LM 181819, GBE 163552 / LM 181819
GBE 163557 / LM 181819, GBE 163559
Rechte Seite: LM 181819, GBE 163566

13

Linke Seite: LM 181819, GBE 163584
Rechte Seite: *(v. l. nach r. u.v. o. nach u.)*
LM 181819, GBE 163564 / LM 181819, GBE 163562
LM 181819, GBE 163565 / LM 181819, GBE 163561
LM 181819, GBE 163569 / LM 181819, GBE 163567

14

Linke Seite: LM 181838, GBE 163938
Rechte Seite: *(v. l. nach r. u. v. o. nach u.)*
LM 181838, GBE 163933 / LM 181838, GBE 163944
LM 181838, GBE 163936 / LM 181838, GBE 163937

15

Linke Seite: *(v. l. nach r. u. v. o. nach u.)*
LM 181822, GBE 162578 / LM 181822, GBE 162566
LM 181822, GBE 162590 / LM 181822, GBE 162547
LM 181822, GBE 162589 / LM 181822, GBE 162589
Rechte Seite: LM 181822, GBE 162578

16

Linke Seite: LM 183735.7
Rechte Seite: *(v. l. nach r. u. v. o. nach u.)*
LM 185227.6 / LM 185227.2 / LM 185227.4 / LM 185227.3

17

Linke Seite: LM 183725.3 / LM 183725.1 / LM 183725.2
LM 183725.4
Rechte Seite: LM 183737.4

18

Linke Seite: *(v. l. nach r. u. v. o. nach u.)*
LM 183723.9 / LM 183723.6 / LM 183723.4 / LM 183723.3
Rechte Seite: *(v. l. nach r. u. v. o. nach u.)*
LM 183723.1 / LM 183723.2 / LM 183723.7 / LM 183723.8

19

Linke Seite: *(v. l. nach r. u. v. o. nach u.)*
LM 183723.5 / LM 183723.11 / LM 183723.10 / LM 183723.12
Rechte Seite: LM 181822, GBE 162555

20

Linke Seite: LM 183728.4
Rechte Seite: LM 181835.1, GBE 163875

21

Linke Seite: *(v. l. nach r. u. v. o. nach u.)*
LM 181840.1 / LM 181840.1, GBE 162973 / LM 181840.1
GBE 163016 / LM 181840.1, GBE 163009 / LM 181840.1
GBE 163000 / LM 181840.1, GBE 16042
Rechte Seite: *(v. o. nach u.)* LM 181840.1, GBE 163014
LM 181840.1, GBE 163022

22

Linke Seite: *(v. o. nach u.)*
LM 181840.1, GBE 163003 / LM 181840.1, GBE 163004
Rechte Seite: *(v. o. nach u.)*
LM 181840.1, GBE 163025 / LM 181840.1, GBE 163026

23

Linke Seite: *(v. o. nach u.)*
LM 181840.1, GBE 163029 / LM 181840.1, GBE 163073
Rechte Seite: LM 181822, GBE 162587

24

Linke Seite: LM 181830.5
Rechte Seite: LM 185244.1 © *MONIKA ROBL*

25

Linke Seite: LM 183767.8-14
Rechte Seite: LM 181839.1, GBE 162950

26

Beide Seiten: LM 181836.33

27

Linke Seite: LM 181836.42
Rechte Seite: LM 181836.43

28

Linke Seite: LM 181836.44
Rechte Seite: LM 181836.46

29

Linke Seite: *(v. l. nach r. u. v. o. nach u.)*
LM 181839.1, GBE 162924 / LM 181839.1, GBE 162925
LM 181839.1, GBE 162936 / LM 181839.1, GBE 162952
LM 181839.1, GBE 162946 / LM 181839.1, GBE 162968
Rechte Seite: *(v. l. nach r. u. v. o. nach u.)*
LM 181839.1, GBE 162931 / LM 181839.1, GBE 162934
LM 181839.1, GBE 162937 / LM 181839.1, GBE 162951

30

Linke Seite: *(v. l. nach r. u. v. o. nach u.)*
LM 181815 / LM 181815, GBE 163447 / LM 181814
GBE 163432 / LM 181815, GBE 163452 / LM 181815
GBE 163448 / LM 181815, GBE 163453
Rechte Seite: LM 181838, GBE 163954

31

Linke Seite: *(v. l. nach r. u. v. o. nach u.)*
LM 181811, GBE 163337 / LM 181811 163338 / LM 181811
GBE 163339 / LM 181811, GBE 163340 / LM 181811, GBE 16341
Rechte Seite: *(v. l. nach r. u. v. o. nach u.)*
LM 181811, GBE 163342 / LM 181811, GBE 163345
LM 181811, GBE 163343 / LM 181811, GBE 163344
LM 181811, GBE 163350 / LM 181811, GBE 163351

32

Linke Seite: LM 181811, GBE 163353
Rechte Seite: LM 181811, GBE 163349

33

Linke Seite: LM 181838. 2, GBE 164754
Rechte Seite: LM 181838.2, GBE 164753

34

Linke Seite: *(v. o. nach u.)*
LM 181822, GBE 162596 / LM 181822, GBE 162597
Rechte Seite: LM 181821, GBE 163101

35

Linke Seite: LM 181821, GBE 163099
Rechte Seite: *(v. o. nach u.)*
LM 181821, GBE 163076 / LM 181821, GBE 163100

36

Linke Seite: *(v. o. nach u.)*
LM 181821, GBE 163098 / LM 181821, GBE 163125
Rechte Seite: LM 181821, GBE 163094

37

Linke Seite: LM 181838, GBE 163990
Rechte Seite: *(v. l. nach r.)*
LM 183723.18 / LM 183723.14

38

Linke Seite: LM 185244.5 © *MONIKA ROBL*
Rechte Seite: LM 183244.6 © *MONIKA ROBL*

39

Linke Seite: LM 181838, GBE 163990
Rechte Seite: *(v. l. nach r. u. v. o. nach u.)*
LM 185229.3 / LM 183229.2 / LM 185229.4 / LM 185229.1

40

Linke Seite: LM 185230.1
Rechte Seite: *(v. l. nach r. u. v. o. nach u.)*
LM 185230.3 / LM 185230.2 / LM 185228.6 / LM 185228.5
LM 185228.4 / LM 185228.3

41

Linke Seite: *(v. o. nach u.)*
LM 181822, GBE 162601 / LM 181822, GBE 162562
Rechte Seite: *(v. l. nach r. u. v. o. nach u.)*
LM 181822, GBE 162 / LM 181822 , GBE 162571 / LM 181822
GBE 162550 / LM 181822, GBE 162550 / LM 181822
GBE 162569 / LM 181822, GBE 162569

42

Beide Seiten: LM 181822, GBE 162575

43

Linke Seite: *(v. o. nach u.)*
LM 181822, GBE 162561 / LM 181822, GBE 162607
Rechte Seite: LM 181822, GBE 162613

44

Linke Seite: LM 181822, GBE 162613
Rechte Seite: *(v. l. nach r. u. v. o. nach u.)*
LM 181822, GBE 162605 / LM 181822, GBE 162605
LM 181822, GBE 162612 / LM 181822, GBE 162612

45

Linke Seite: LM 183723.19
Rechte Seite: LM 181822, GBE 162604

46

Linke Seite: *(v. l. nach r. u. v. o. nach u.)*
LM 181812, GBE 163360 / LM 181812, GBE 163394
LM 181812, GBE 163396 / LM 181812, GBE 163399
LM 181812, GBE 163398
Rechte Seite: *(v. l. nach r. u. v. o. nach u.)*
LM 181812, GBE 163362 / LM 181812, GBE 163368
LM 181812, GBE 163365 / LM 181812, GBE 163375
LM 181812, GBE 163379 / LM 181812, GBE 163386

47

Beide Seiten: LM 181810

48

Linke Seite: LM 181812, GBE 163402 / LM 181812, GBE 163403
Rechte Seite: LM 181824, GBE 162848

49

Linke Seite: LM 181824
Rechte Seite: *(v. l. nach r. u. v. o. nach u.)*
LM 181824.8 / LM 181824.28 / LM 181824.29 / LM 181824.30

50

Linke Seite: LM 181824.1 / LM 181824.5 / LM 181824.2
LM 181824.20
Rechte Seite: LM 181824.31 / LM 181824.32 / LM 181824.14
LM 181824.15

51

Linke Seite: *(v. l. nach r.)* LM 181824.42 / LM 181824.43
Rechte Seite: (v. l. nach r.) LM 181824.21 / LM 181824.33

52

Linke Seite: *(v. l. nach r. u. v. o. nach u.)*
LM 181824.52 / LM 181824.51 / LM 181824.50 / LM 181824.49
Rechte Seite: *(v. l. nach r. u. v. o. nach u.)*
LM 181824.26 / LM 181824.27 / LM 181824.38 / LM 181824.37

53

Linke Seite: LM 181838, GBE 163979
Rechte Seite: LM 185244.8 © *MONIKA ROBL*

54

Linke Seite: LM 181823.2 GBE 163641
Rechte Seite: LM 183702.5

55

Linke Seite:LM 183702.18
Rechte Seite: LM 183702.19

56

Linke Seite: LM 181838, GBE 163993
Rechte Seite: LM 183702.13

57

Linke Seite: LM 183701.70
Rechte Seite: LM 183701.69

58

Beide Seiten: LM 184190.1

59

Linke Seite: LM 183701.71
Rechte Seite: LM 183713

60

Linke Seite: *(von l. nach r. u. pro Streifen)*
1. Streifen: *(v. o. nach u.)* LM 18368626-30
2. Streifen: *(v. o. nach u.)* LM 183686.31-35
3. Streifen: *(v. o. nach u.)* LM 185686.19-21
Rechte Seite: *(v. l. nach r. u. v. o. nach u.)*
LM 183686.3 / LM 183686.4 / LM 183686.7 / LM 183686.5

61

Linke Seite: *(v. o. nach u.)*
LM 183686.84 / LM 183723.13 / LM 184190.2
Rechte Seite: LM 183696.2

62

Linke Seite: LM 181940.41
Rechte Seite: *(v. l. nach r. u. v. o. nach u.)*
LM 183702.8 / LM 181838, GBE 163965 / LM 183696.2
LM 181838, GBE 163965

63

Linke Seite: *(v. l. nach r. u. v. o. nach u.)*
LM 181816 / LM 181816, GBE 163467 / LM 181816
GBE 163468 / LM 181816, GBE 163488 / LM 181816
GBE 163484 / LM 181816, GBE 163475
Rechte Seite: *(v. l. nach r. u. v. o. nach u.)*
LM 181816, GBE 163492 / LM 181816, GBE 163473
LM 181816, GBE 163486 / LM 181816, GBE 163485
LM 181816, GBE 163469 / LM 181816, GBE 163476

64

Linke Seite: LM 181816, GBE 163479
Rechte Seite: LM 183688.1

65

Linke Seite: LM 183688.2
Rechte Seite: *(v. l. nach r. u. v. o. nach u.)*
LM 181816, GBE 163478 / LM 181816, GBE 163477
LM 181816, GBE 163470 / LM 181816, GBE 163470

66

Linke Seite: *(v. l. nach r. u. v. o. nach u.)*
LM 183693.4 / LM 183693.3 / LM 183693.1 / LM 183693.2
Rechte Seite: LM 183690.1

67

Linke Seite: LM 184188
Rechte Seite: LM 184189

68

Linke Seite: (von *(v. l. nach r. u. v. o. nach u.)*
LM 181827.32 / LM 181827.31 / LM 181827.29 / LM 181827.33
Rechte Seite: *(v. l. nach r. u. v. o. nach u.)*
LM 181827.17 / LM 181827.13 / LM 181827.18 / LM 181827.1

69

Linke Seite: LM 183703.40
Rechte Seite: *(v. l. nach r. u. v. o. nach u.)*
LM 183703.39 / LM 183703.37 / LM 183703.38

70

Linke Seite: LM 183704.2
Rechte Seite: *(v. l. nach r. u. v. o. nach u.)*
LM 181827.39 / LM 181827.40 / LM 183704.1 / LM 181827.42

71

Linke Seite: *(von l. nach r. u. pro Streifen)*
1. Streifen: *(v. o. nach u.)*
LM 183704.25-27 / LM 183690.16-17 / LM 183690.11-14
2. Streifen: *(v. o. nach u.)*
LM 183704.9-12 / LM 183704.19-22 / LM 183704.28
3. Streifen: *(v. o. nach u.)*
LM 183704.68-69 / LM 183704.59-62 / LM 133704 LM / 183704.56-58
4. Streifen: *(v. o. nach u.)*
LM 183697.27-30 / LM .17-19 / LM 183697.6
Rechte Seite: *(von l. nach r. u. pro Streifen)*
1. Streifen: *(v. o. nach u.)*
LM 183690.36-38 / LM 183698.21-26
2. Streifen: *(v. o. nach u.)*
LM 183686.40-46 LM 183686.49-50
3. Streifen: *(v. o. nach u.)*
LM 183703.4-7 / LM 183703.9-10 / LM 183703.17-19
4. Streifen: *(v. o. nach u.)*
LM 183703.22-25 / LM 183703.27-30 / LM 183703.20

72

Linke Seite: LM 183689.2
Rechte Seite: LM 183687.1

73

Linke Seite: LM 183702.16
Rechte Seite: *(v. l. nach r. u. v. o. nach u.)*
LM 183696.7 / LM 181830.42 / LM 181830.43 / LM 183702.6

74

Linke Seite: LM 181838, GBE 163976
Rechte Seite: *(v. o. nach u.)*
LM 183686.89 / LM 183686.90

75

Linke Seite: LM 181840.1, GBE 163050
Rechte Seite: LM 183686.82

76

Beide Seiten: LM 185238.1 © *ROLAND REITER*

77

Linke Seite: LM 185239.1
Rechte Seite: LM 185244.2 © *MONIKA ROBL*

78

Linke Seite: LM 181830.35
Rechte Seite: LM 181830.40

79

Linke Seite: LM 181828.76
Rechte Seite: LM 181830.11

80

Linke Seite: LM 181835.1, GBE 163904
Rechte Seite: *(v. l. nach r. u. v. o. nach u.)*
LM 181835.1, GBE 163905 / LM 181835.1, GBE 163904
LM 181835.5 / LM 181835.1, GBE 163903

81

Linke Seite: LM 181835.8
Rechte Seite: LM 181835.1, GBE 163903 / LM 181835.1
GBE 163903 / LM 181835.7 / LM 181835.7

82

Linke Seite: LM 181835.1, GBE 163866
Rechte Seite: LM 181835.7

83

Linke Seite: LM 181835.1, GBE 163901
Rechte Seite: LM 181835.1, GBE 163884

84

Linke Seite: LM 181835.1, GBE 163898
Rechte Seite: LM 181835.1, GBE 163892

85

Linke Seite: *(v. o. nach u.)*
LM 181835.1 / LM 181835.1, GBE 163907 *(gelbe Seite)*
LM 181835.1, GBE 163908
Rechte Seite: LM 181835.1, GBE 163899 *(gelbe Seite)*
LM 181835.1, GBE 163900 / LM 181835.1, GBE 163895
(gelbe Seite) LM 181835.1, GBE 163896 *(rote Seite)*

86

Linke Seite: LM 181835.1, GBE 163890 / LM 181835.1
GBE 163890 / LM 181835.1, GBE 163893 / LM 181835.1
GBE 163893
Rechte Seite: *(v. o. nach u.)*
LM 181835.1, GBE 163885 *(gelbe Seite)* / LM 181835.1
GBE 163886, *(rote Seite)* / LM 181835.1, GBE 163883
(gelbe Seite) / LM 181835.1, GBE 163884 *(rote Seite)*

87

Linke Seite: *(v. l. nach r. u.v. o. nach u.)*
LM 181835.1, GBE 163889 / LM 181835.1, GBE 163889
LM 181835.1, GBE 163890 / LM 181835.1, GBE 163890
Rechte Seite: LM 1818353.1, GBE 163881

88

Linke Seite: LM 181834.2, GBE 163838
Rechte Seite: LM 181828.15

89

Linke Seite: *(v. o. nach u.)*
LM 181832.2 / LM 181832.3
Rechte Seite: *(v. l. nach r. u. v. o. nach u.)*
LM 181832.7 / LM 181832.8 / LM 181832.11 / LM 181832.12

90

Linke Seite: LM 181835.7
Rechte Seite: LM 181835.6

91

Rechte Seite: LM 181829.57

92

Linke Seite: LM 181837.1
Rechte Seite: LM 181830.9

93

Linke Seite: LM 181837.33
Rechte Seite: LM 181837.26 / LM 181837.29 / LM 181837.30
LM 181837.31

94

Rechte Seite: LM 181825.53

95

Rechte Seite: LM 183721.92-109

96

Beide Seiten: LM 183721.113-147

97

Linke Seite: LM 181840.1, GBE 162999 / LM 181840.1
GBE 163053 / LM181840.1, GBE 163057

98

IMPRESSUM / IMPRINT

Herausgegeben von Sturm & Drang Publishers und dem Schweizerischen Nationalmuseum anlässlich der Ausstellung «wild und schön – Mode von Ursula Rodel» im Landesmuseum Zürich, 21.7.2023 – 31.3.2024.

Published by Sturm & Drang Publishers and Swiss National Museum on the occasion of the exhibition «wild and beautiful – fashion by Ursula Rodel» at the National Museum Zurich, 21.7.2023 – 31.3.2024.

© 2023 für diese erste Auflage Schweizerisches Nationalmuseum und Sturm & Drang Publishers, alle Rechte vorbehalten.

© 2023 for this first edition Swiss National Museum and Sturm & Drang Publishers, all rights reserved.

© 2023 alle Bilder, wenn nicht anders vermerkt: Ursula Rodel / Schweizerisches Nationalmuseum.

© 2023 all images, if not otherwise noted: Ursula Rodel / Swiss National Museum.

«ever fallen in love» Songtext mit freundlicher Genehmigung von / lyrics used with kind permission of Pete Shelley estate.

Projektleitung / Project managers:
Christina Sonderegger, Reto Caduff, Chris Eggli

Bildkonzept und Gestaltung / Visual concept and design:
Chris Eggli, chriseggli.ch

Redaktion / Editor: Christina Sonderegger

Lektorat und Übersetzung / Copy editing and translation:
Sturm & Drang Publishers

Scans: Zvonimir Pisonic

Bildbearbeitung / Retouching: Chris Eggli

Inventar und Rechteabklärung / Inventory and Rights clearance:
Noemi Albert

Gedruckt bei / Printed at: Wanderer Druck

ISBN 978-3-905875-62-1 (SNM), ISBN 978-3-906822-49-5 (S & D)

Vertrieb / Distributed by: idea books, antenne books (GB)

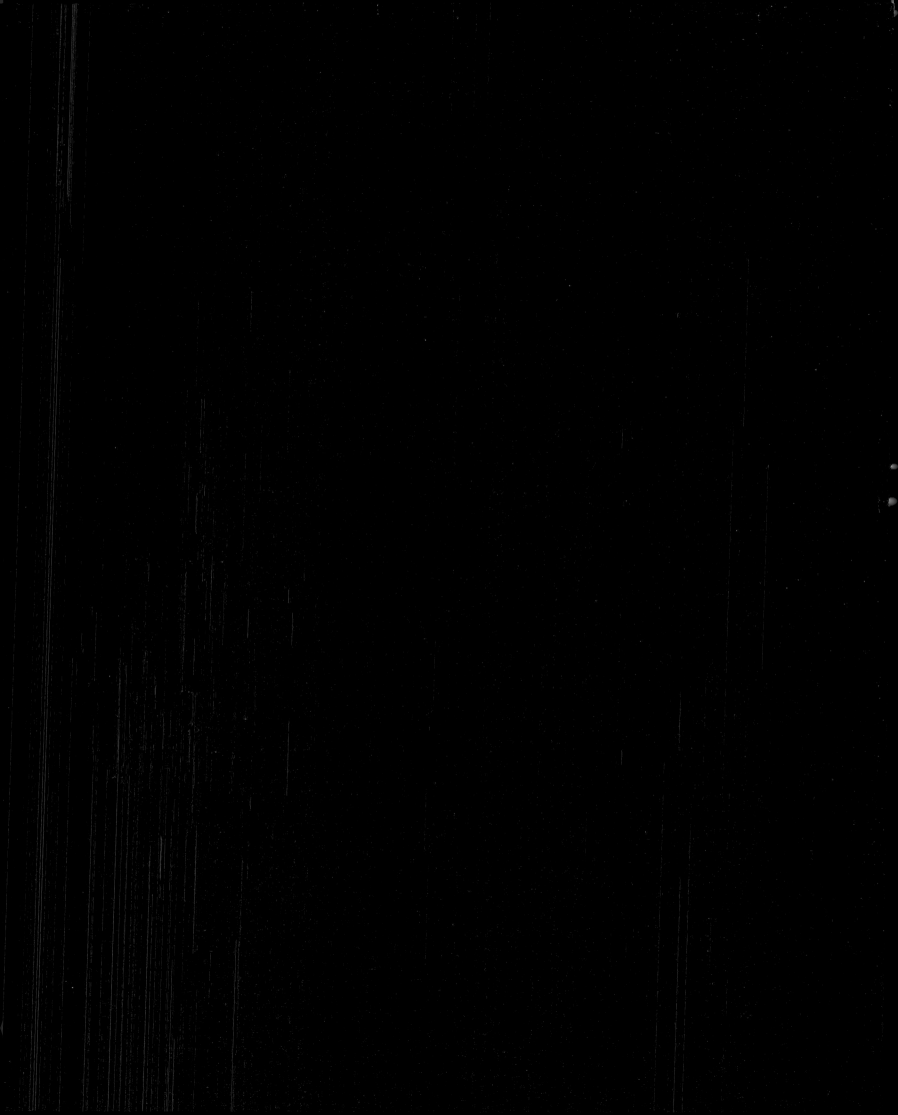

DANK / ACKNOWLEDGMENTS

Katharina Bébié-Lardelli
This Brunner
Jacqueline Burckhardt
Christoph Bürge
Bice Curiger
Catherine Deneuve
Gérard Depardieu
Ruth Grüninger
Joya Indermühle
Ursina Lüthi-Bossard
Christina Ruchti-Rodel
Zoë Stähli
Edi Stöckli
Kai-Peter Uhlig
Brigitte Weiss
Sissi Zöbeli

Sturm & Drang Publishers
Wolfbachstrasse 11, CH-8032 Zürich
sturmanddrang.net

Schweizerisches Nationalmuseum
Museumstrasse 2, Postfach, CH-8021 Zürich
nationalmuseum.ch